W9-CAA-787

Dealing With...
WHEN PEOPLE DIE

by Jane Lacey

Illustrated by Venitia Dean

PowerKiDS press

Published in 2019 by **The Rosen Publishing Group, Inc.**
29 East 21st Street, New York, NY 10010

Cataloging-in-Publication Data

Names: Lacey, Jane. | Dean, Venitia, illustrator.
Title: When people die / Jane Lacey; illustrated by Venitia Dean.
Description: New York : PowerKids Press, 2019. | Series: Dealing with... | Includes glossary and index.
Identifiers: LCCN ISBN 9781538339152 (pbk.) | ISBN 9781538339145 (library bound) | ISBN 9781538339169 (6 pack)
Subjects: LCSH: Children and death--Juvenile literature. | Grief in children--Juvenile literature. | Death--Psychological aspects--Juvenile literature.
Classification: LCC BF723.D3 L33 2019 | DDC 155.9'37083--dc23

Editor: Sarah Peutrill
Series Design: Collaborate

Manufactured in the United States of America

CPSIA Compliance Information: Batch #CS18PK: For Further Information contact Rosen Publishing, New York, New York at 1-800-237-9932.

Contents

I DON'T KNOW WHAT'S HAPPENING!

Lola's granny has died but her family hasn't told her yet. They stop talking when she comes into the room. Lola feels worried and afraid. She doesn't know what is going on, but she knows it is something bad.

Ewan is Lola's big brother

Lola keeps asking me, "Where's Granny? What's happened?" I want to tell her, but Mom and Dad say Lola's too young to understand about Granny dying. But not knowing is making Lola feel unhappy.

Granny was staying with us because she was ill. Mom was looking after her. One evening, there was lots of running around, whispering, and phone calls. No one would tell me what was happening. Mom asked me to stay in my bedroom.

I saw an ambulance from my bedroom window. They took Granny away. Mom says Granny isn't coming back, but she won't tell me why. What's happened to Granny? Are they whispering because they don't want me to know that Granny doesn't love us anymore?

What can Lola do?

Lola is worrying because she doesn't know what's happened to her granny. She can:

★ tell her mom she is worried
★ ask why Granny has gone away
★ say not knowing is making her think frightening things

What Lola did

I told Mom I thought Granny wasn't coming back because she didn't love us. So Mom gave me a hug and told me Granny had died. I burst into tears because I'll never see Granny again. Mom said Granny loved us and her love will never leave us.

I feel a bit better, but I wish Granny was still here.

WHAT IS DEATH?

Death is when someone's body stops working and can't be made better.

Death is a natural part of life. All living things — plants, animals, and people — grow older and eventually die one day. Living things don't live forever.

People die because their body gets old and worn out. They die because they are too sick to get better. Sometimes people die because they have a very bad accident. A dead body can't feel pain or know what's going on.

I DON'T WANT TO SAY GOODBYE!

Tim finds it hard to believe his dad has died. He won't go to the funeral to say goodbye because he wants to think he will see his dad again.

George

Tim

George is Tim's friend

I know Tim's dad has died, but he keeps talking about him as if he is still alive. He got really mad at me when I said I was sorry about his dad.

Tim's story

Dad hasn't been healthy for a long time. He's had medicine and operations, and they've always made him feel better! But Mom says that Dad got too sick for the medicine to work anymore. She says Dad died.

I can't believe Dad died. I think if I don't say goodbye to Dad and don't go to the funeral, he'll walk in the door again, smiling! I'm afraid if I say goodbye, I really will never see him again.

It would help Tim to accept that his dad has passed away. He can:

* ★ talk to his mom about it and listen to what she says
* ★ go to his dad's funeral and say goodbye
* ★ write a goodbye letter

What Tim did

I told Mom I didn't want Dad to be dead. We both cried together. Mom said I could write Dad a letter. She said people who loved Dad would be at his funeral. We would all remember him and say goodbye. I'm going to the funeral. It helps to think I won't be the only one saying goodbye.

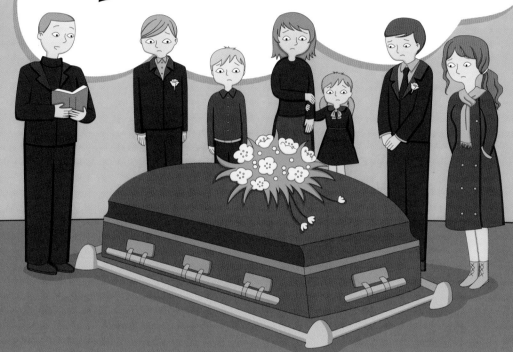

WHAT HAPPENS AT A FUNERAL?

At a funeral, the person who has died is put in a wooden box called a coffin. Their body is either buried, which means put in the ground, or it is cremated, which means burned. Their name is written on a gravestone, a plaque, or in a special book of remembrance.

Family and friends of the person who has died get together to remember them and say goodbye.

A religious service or ceremony may be held.

11

I'M ANGRY WITH MY BROTHER FOR LEAVING ME

Wes's older brother Henry died in an accident. Wes feels angry with his brother for leaving him on his own and making his mom and dad unhappy.

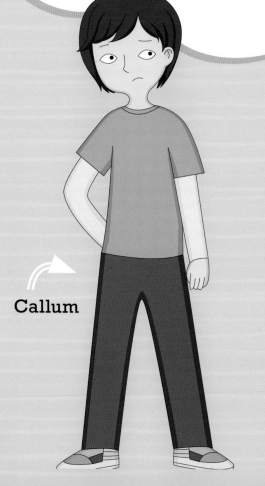

Callum

Callum is Wes's friend

Since Henry died, Wes is angry all the time — with Henry for dying and with his mom and dad about everything! He gets really angry if I talk about my big brother. I can't say anything right!

Wes's story

A car knocked my big brother Henry off his bike and hurt him so badly he died.

I'm angry with Henry. I keep thinking he should have been more careful!

Now Mom and Dad are sad all the time. I can't talk about Henry because it makes them even sadder.

And they worry about me. They keep saying, "Be careful, Wes!" They won't let me ride my bike anymore.

My friend Callum's big brother is alive, but mine is dead. It's not fair!

Wes

13

Wes's mom and dad feel sad and worried because of Henry's accident. Wes can talk to a grown-up he trusts. He can:

★ say he feels angry with Henry
★ say he knows his mom and dad worry about him
★ say he doesn't like it when they think he is going to have an accident, too

What Wes did

I talked to Uncle Pete and he talked to Mom and Dad. Now they let me ride my bike in the park. I'm taking a cycling test so I will know how to stay safe when I ride on the road. I think Mom and Dad will always worry about me more because of what happened to Henry.

WILL I EVER STOP FEELING SAD?

Emily's mom died a year ago, but Emily often feels sad still. She wonders if she will ever be happy again.

Molly

Emily

Molly is Emily's friend

Sometimes when Emily and I are having fun and she's laughing and happy, she suddenly gets sad and won't play anymore. I know she's thinking about her mom, but she won't talk about it.

Emily's story

Wednesday is the anniversary of Mom's death. It's a whole year since she died, but I still feel sad.

Every time I do something I used to do with Mom, I miss her and feel like crying because she isn't here anymore. I cried when Dad helped me make my birthday cake because Mom and I always did it together. Dad cried, too.

Sometimes I forget that Mom has died and I feel happy. Then I remember and I feel sad again.

What can Emily do?

Emily will always miss her mom. It helps to have happy memories. She can:

★ tell her friend Molly how she feels
★ talk to her dad
★ plan to do something on the anniversary of her mom's death so that it isn't just a sad day

What Emily did

I talked to Dad and he said he still feels sad, too. We decided to make Wednesday a special day for Mom. We cooked her favorite meal, went on her favorite walk, and even told her favorite jokes! We'll always be sad that Mom died, but we don't always have to be sad when we remember her.

I'M AFRAID I WILL DIE, TOO

Luke thought that only pets and very old people died. So when his friend Max died, he was shocked. Now Luke is afraid of dying, too.

Jack

Jack is Luke's friend

Luke and Max were my best friends. Max died because he was very sick. Now Luke thinks he's going to die, too. But just because Max died, it doesn't mean Luke or I are going to die.

Luke

Luke's story

I was sad when my pet hamster died, and I cried when Gram died. But I didn't worry because hamsters don't live for very long and Gram was very old.

Then Max died. He was only a kid like me! Now I think about dying all the time. I worry that Mom and Dad will die. I worry that I will die. I can't get to sleep. When I do, I have nightmares. I go into Mom and Dad's room to make sure they are okay.

Jack keeps saying, "Of course you won't die!" He gets fed up with me. I don't want to tell Mom and Dad in case they get fed up with me, too. I wish I didn't feel so afraid.

What can Luke do?

Worrying about dying is making Luke unhappy. He can:

★ tell his mom and dad he is afraid of dying
★ say he is afraid they will die

What Luke did

I told Mom and Dad. They said everyone has to die at some point, but there was no reason to think any of us would die soon. They said I must tell them when I feel afraid. But I don't feel so afraid now that I've talked to them. I do miss Max, though.

MY PARENTS DON'T LOVE ME ANYMORE

Sophia's mom and dad are sad that baby Layla died. Sophia thinks they loved baby Layla more than they love her.

Sophia

Priti

Priti is Sophia's friend

Sophia told me her mom and dad talk about her sister Layla all the time. She thinks they wish she had died and not Layla. She tries to be good so they will love her more. But I said, "Our moms and dads love us when we're good and when we're bad."

Sophia's story

Layla died when she was only a baby. Mom and Dad talk about how sweet and good she was. They say, "Layla would have been a lovely girl."

I'm not sweet and good all the time. Sometimes I'm naughty. So I think Mom and Dad wish Layla was alive instead of me.

I try to be good so they'll love me and be glad I didn't die. Sometimes, I feel angry with Layla. I feel bad about that.

What can Sophia do?

- ★ remember that her mom and dad love her and would never wish she had died instead
- ★ tell her mom and dad how she feels.

What Sophia did

I told Mom and Dad I thought they wished it was me and not Layla who had died. I said I would try to be good. They gave me a big hug and said they loved me all the time — even when I was naughty. They don't wish Layla was alive instead of me. Now that I know they love me, I'm not angry with Layla anymore.

I MISS GRANDPA, TOO

Jayden thinks no one knows how much he misses his grandpa. Jayden's grandpa was very popular with his family and friends. They are all sad he died, but Jayden is very sad, too.

Ali

Ali is Jayden's friend

I know Jayden really misses his grandpa. His mom, dad, aunts, and uncles all help each other when they feel sad. I try to help Jayden when he feels sad.

Jayden

Jayden's story

Grandpa was my dad's father. Everyone loved him. He had lots of stories to tell and he was kind and funny. He called me his "little pal" and we did things together.

When he died, everyone was sad — Dad, Mom, my uncles and aunts, and Grandpa's friends. When they get together to remember Grandpa, I feel left out.

I miss Grandpa just as much as they do.

I'm afraid if I talk to Dad or Mom about Grandpa, it will make them sad all over again.

25

He can:

★ talk to his friend Ali
★ talk to his mom and dad or his aunts or uncles
★ tell them he misses his grandpa and that he feels left out

What Jayden did

I talked to Ali. He said the grown-ups would understand that I missed Grandpa, too. So I talked to Grandpa's sister. She is making a book with photographs and letters and stories about Grandpa, and I'm helping her. We put something new in the book when we feel sad about Grandpa, and it helps us feel a bit better.

HOW CAN I REMEMBER SOMEONE SPECIAL?

Someone who has died can always be part of you. Remember:

★ special things they did and said
★ happy times together
★ games and jokes you shared
★ books, TV shows, and movies you both enjoyed

You could also:

★ make a photo album
★ make a box of memories. Put in things such as a card they sent to you, a scarf they wore, or their favorite poem.
★ help to raise money for charity in their memory
★ plant a tree for them and watch it grow

WHEN OUR FRIEND DIED

When Caitlin and Logan's friend Ruby died, they were shocked and very sad.

Caitlin and Logan's story

Caitlin: When our dog Sandy died, I was really sad that I wouldn't see him again. I never thought the same thing could happen to one of my friends.

Logan: When Ruby died, I was really shocked. I thought only old people died.

Caitlin: Logan and I were Ruby's best friends. Ruby's mom and dad asked if we wanted to go to Ruby's funeral. I wasn't sure. I'd never been to a funeral.

Logan: Caitlin asked me if I wanted to go. I wasn't sure either, but I'm really glad we went.

Caitlin: At Ruby's funeral, her mom and dad, her big brother, and our teacher all talked about Ruby and how special she was.

Logan: All the kids in our class wrote something for Ruby. There were letters, poems, stories, and even jokes.

Caitlin: Her mom and dad read some of them aloud at the funeral. Then they put them with the flowers and cards people had sent.

Logan: Ruby's mom and dad said they were happy we had come to the funeral.

Caitlin: I felt really sad when I got home, and I cried. Mom gave me a hug and said I would begin to feel better, but it might take a long time.

Logan: At school, we planted a tree for Ruby. I think about her every time I see it.

Caitlin: Now we don't feel sad about Ruby all the time. We are often happy and have fun, but it doesn't mean that we have forgotten Ruby.

GLOSSARY

Accident
Something that happens suddenly and unexpectedly. Some very bad accidents can hurt or even kill people.

Afraid
You are afraid when you feel worried about something bad happening.

Alive
People, plants and animals are all alive. When you are alive you move, eat, sleep, learn, and grow.

Ambulance
A van with special equipment that takes people to and from the hospital.

Anniversary
An anniversary is when you remember something that happened on the same date every year. Your birthday is the anniversary of the day you were born.

Die
When someone dies, they are not alive anymore.

Funeral
A funeral takes place when somebody dies and their body is buried or cremated.

Miss
You miss someone when you feel sad that you don't see them anymore.

Sad
You are sad when you feel unhappy. When you feel sad you sometimes want to cry.

Worry
You worry when you don't know what is going to happen and you think something bad might happen.

FURTHER INFORMATION

Books

Amanda Edwards and Leslie Ponciano. *The Elephant in the Room: A Childrens' Book for Grief and Loss*. CreateSpace Independent Publishing Platform, 2014.

Rowland, Joanna. *The Memory Box: A Book About Grief*. Sparkhouse, 2017.

Sornson, Bob. *Stand in My Shoes: Kids Learning About Empathy*. Love and Logic Press, 2013.

PowerKids Press has developed an online list of websites related to the subject of this book. This site is updated regularly. Please use this link to access the list: www.powerkidslinks.com/dw/whenpeopledie

INDEX